THE PRINCE & THE LUTE

Copyright © 1979 Nord-Süd Verlag, Mönchaltorf, Switzerland
First published in Switzerland under the title Der Prinz und die Laute
English text copyright © 1980 Victor Gollancz Ltd.
Copyright English language edition under the imprint
North-South Books © 1986 Rada Matija AG, Staefa, Switzerland

First published in the United States in 1986 by North-South Books, an
imprint of Rada Matija AG.

Distributed in the United States by
Holt, Rinehart and Winston, 383 Madison Avenue,
New York, New York, 10017.
Library of Congress Catalog Card Number 85-63300

ISBN 0-03-008018-5

Printed in Germany

THE PRINCE & THE LUTE

Story by Kurt Baumann/Illustrations by Jean Claverie

North-South Books
New York

Once upon a time there was a prince who wanted peace more than anything else in the world. But his father, the King, had been waging war with a neighbouring king for many years.

The prince spent most of his time in the garden of the royal palace, listening to the song of the birds.

"You are lucky," he sighed. "You are free, while I am expected to lead my men into battle and to burden my people with taxes."

While the prince talked to the birds, the King and his lords surveyed the kingdom from the battlements of the castle. The red silk of the King's gown reached his feet and his golden chain glittered in the sun. In the distance the castle of the neighbouring king could be seen, already in shadow. The King smiled maliciously.

"Your sun, Ottokar, is already setting, while here in my kingdom it is at its height."

The King's lords smiled approvingly. They enjoyed riding to war with King Ottokar. But they frowned when they looked down into the garden and saw the prince sitting there.

"What will happen when our King dies?" they wondered. "The prince is a dreamer and unfit to be a king."

Many years passed. The old King had died and the country was still at war. In the castle grounds the prince paced up and down, but the song of the birds no longer comforted him. His heart was filled with grief and sorrow. He watched the people passing by in the road. They were poorly dressed and their faces were marked by poverty and hunger.

"They have never had a good life," thought the prince, "and now they do not even have enough to eat. They should be ploughing the fields instead of having to march into battle."

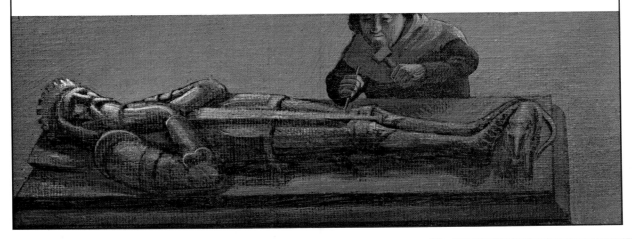

As the prince stood watching the road, he saw a beggar. He called to the beggar, and led him to the well in the courtyard. They looked at their reflections in the water. They looked so alike that they could have been twins.

The prince eyed the beggar's ragged clothes and said, "I shall end this war."

The beggar smiled. "I know that you do not like war, but you will not be able to end it without using force."

"Tomorrow I shall ride to King Ottokar," the prince replied, "and I shall give him all the gold that is left in our kingdom. Surely he will make peace then."

Putting his hand on the prince's shoulder, the beggar said, "We shall meet again." Then he left the garden.

Early the following morning the prince summoned his attendants and had a cart loaded with gold: golden jugs, plates, spoons—anything made of gold that could be found in the palace. Then the prince laid down his sword and ordered his men to do likewise.

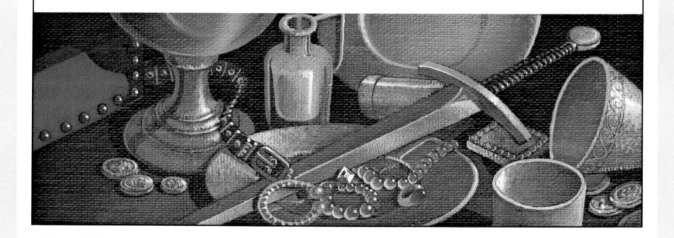

They set off, and on the following day reached King Ottokar's castle. But King Ottokar would not open the gate to them. They could hear his scornful laughter when the fool leant over the battlements to mock them.

The gate remained shut. Sadly the prince turned his horse and he and his men rode back to their own country, weary and travel-stained.

Night was falling as the riders crossed the frontier. It was frosty and the men lit a fire to warm themselves. One after another they fell asleep. The prince alone lay awake, gazing up at the moon.

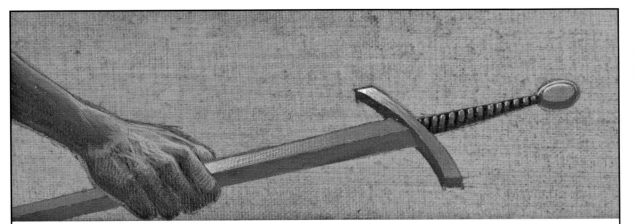

After a while he got up and walked through the forest until he came to a clearing. In the moonlight he saw a ragged figure leaning against a tree and recognised his friend the beggar.

The beggar was holding a sword, and handing it to the prince he said, "There is no other way. You must fight to end this war."

The prince stamped his foot. "I will not fight."

The beggar sighed. "Soon you will be King," he said. "Your country needs peace."

Suddenly the prince cried, "You are bolder than I. You shall be King in my place."

They exchanged their clothes and, smiling at one another, they embraced. Before sunrise the prince left the forest and went into the mountains.

The prince wandered through the mountains for many days until he reached a lonely hut. He decided to spend the rest of his life in this remote wilderness.

He mended the leaking roof, looked for wood to light a fire on the hearth, and gathered berries and wild honey. Most of the time, however, he spent sitting in front of his hut, listening to the song of the birds. After a while he learnt to distinguish them: the finches, the sparrows, the larks, the nightingales, the blackbirds.

"If one could only imitate them," the prince thought. "The birds are happier than people."

The prince lived in the mountains for a long time. One day the beggar came to see him. He was now King, and he had roamed the country for days looking for the prince. The prince embraced him like a brother. Then he looked at him closely. The beggar seemed to have become much older. His cheeks were hollow, his face lined. Only his eyes were still young, and the light shone in them.

"You have withdrawn from the world, as you always wanted to," the King said, envy in his voice.

The prince laughed. "I am very grateful to you. You have given me all this."

"I have defeated Ottokar," the King told him. "It was not easy. But now what can be done with the prisoners? My lords advise me to kill them."

The prince thought for a while. Then he said, "You were bold in your campaigns. Be merciful now. Give them freedom."

Another year passed, and once again the King came to the prince's hut.

"The country is in dire need," he said. "The poor are hungry, and the rich will give them nothing to eat."

The prince was silent for a bit, then he said, "Be brave enough to be a friend of the poor, too. Give them land, and tools to till the land, and seeds, so that they can get what they need from their own fields."

Years passed and the country slowly recovered. The prince, unaware of this, lived in his hut, listening to the song of the birds. They were not afraid to pick berries from his hand. They would sit on his shoulder and talk to him in strange voices. The prince was happy, although sometimes he worried about the poor in the kingdom. However, he knew that a good king was watching over them.

One day the King visited him again. They greeted one another like true friends and the King said, "You know, all now goes well in the kingdom. The poor live off their crops and dress themselves in wool and velvet. The prisoners have been set free and do not wish to return to their own country. The rich have lost some of their land, but they have learnt to put up with it."

"So why did you come to see me, since everybody is happy," the prince asked, puzzled.

"That's just it," sighed the King. "I know that the people are not really happy. Now that everybody has enough, they all envy their neighbours for what they have."

The prince was lost in deep thought. When the sun had almost set, he rose and took some thin shingles from the roof of his hut. Then he cut the resin from a tree and, joining the shingles together, he made a small box.

"This is the world," he said.

Then with a red hot ember he burnt a hole in the box.

"And this is poverty. Look, there is nothing but emptiness and darkness."

The King watched him closely.

Now the prince set a wooden bridge across the hole. "This stands for the possessions that could change want and misery. But people are still not happy."

He cut several strips from a ram's gut which was drying above the door. Then he twisted the strips and tightened them over the bridge and the opening. When his hand touched the strings, a strange, bright music sounded.

"Take these sounds to the people," the hermit said to the King who was listening in amazement. "Those who sing and play and dance will forget their envy."

The King took the gift in his hands with great care, embraced the prince, and went away.

When the prince was alone again, he thought about human envy and quarrelsomeness. The lute would surely help people to be happier, even though the music would never sound quite as beautiful as the song of the birds.

Jean Claverie was born in 1946 and grew up in Beaune, France. He was trained at the Academy of Art in Lyon, France and in Geneva, Switzerland. After teaching for many years at the National School of Art in Lyon and working as an illustrator he started to illustrate children's books. Jean Claverie is married to an illustrator, and they have two children.

Kurt Baumann was born in Switzerland in 1935. After training as a goldsmith, he worked as a farm laborer in Norway. Several jobs later, he went to a university where he studied history, German language and literature and teaching. He has written many plays and picture books for children as well as poetry. Kurt Baumann is married and has two children.